Double Trouble

Adapted by Jenne Simon

fro SOU... ...rtigan

© Spin Master Charming Productions Inc., 2014, All rights reserved. ® and © Nelvana Limited.
™Corus Entertainment Inc. All rights reserved. Used under license by Scholastic Inc.

Scholastic Children's Books,
Euston House, 24 Eversholt Street,
London NW1 1DB, UK

A division of Scholastic Ltd
London ~ New York ~ Toronto ~ Sydney ~ Auckland
Mexico City ~ New Delhi ~ Hong Kong

First published in the US by Scholastic Inc, 2016
SCHOLASTIC and associated logos are trademarks and/or registered trademarks of Scholastic Inc.
Published in the UK by Scholastic Ltd, 2016

ISBN 978 1407 16407 6

Printed in Malaysia

2 4 6 8 10 9 7 5 3 1

Papers used by Scholastic Children's Books are made from woods grown in sustainable forests.

www.scholastic.co.uk

It was morning in Charmville. Hazel was looking everywhere for her favourite pillow. She and the other Little Charmers were having a sleepover at the Charmhouse that night.

"Goblins and toads!" cried Hazel's dad when he saw the mess. "What's this?"

Hazel raised her wand. It was time to try a new spell!

Hidden somewhere in my room, find my pillow— make it ZOOM!

It worked! But her dad wasn't too happy when her pillow hit him in the face.

"You can't go anywhere until you clean your room and finish your homework," he said. "And no magic, okay? I'd like it to be all you."

"Okay." Hazel sighed.

Hazel turned to her magic mirror. Her best friends Lavender and Posie appeared on the surface.

"Bad news, Charmers," Hazel said. "I can't come to the sleepover until I finish my homework *and* clean my room."

"Then we're coming over to help," said Lavender.

When Lavender and Posie saw their friend's room, they realized it was more than just a mess.

"This is a Hazel-sized disaster!" cried Lavender.

"How's your homework going?" asked Posie.

"Just one spell left to learn — the Make It Double spell," said Hazel.

"Hey, I have an idea!" Hazel exclaimed. "I can use this spell to make a copy of myself and have 'me' clean up! Then we can go to the sleepover."

A-bibbity whirl! Make an exact copy of this girl!

Magically, an exact copy of Hazel appeared!

"I guess that means I finished my homework," joked Hazel.

Posie looked worried. "Didn't your dad say *you're* supposed to do the cleaning?"

"He said it had to be all me," Hazel replied. "And now there are two of me!"

Hazel smiled at her copy. "Can you please clean my room so I can go to a sleepover?"

"How much do you want me to clean?" Hazel Two asked.

"If it's messy, clean it," said the real Hazel. "Clean everything. Thanks, me!" She turned to Lavender and Posie. "To the Charmhouse!"

The girls had a twinkling good time at their sleepover.

They made some sparktastic popcorn.

They had a magical pillow fight.

They even made funny shadow creatures on the walls.

But Hazel wondered how things were going back home.

Hazel Two had been busy. The real Hazel's bedroom was spotless.
"Great work!" said Hazel's dad. "Now you can go to the sleepover."
"No. I still have to clean everything," Hazel Two said seriously.

"Dirty dishes or dirty laundry . . . I cannot do these at the same time,"
Hazel Two said. Then she spotted Hazel's textbook. It was open to the
Make It Double spell. So the copy copied herself!

"Greetings, Hazel!" said Hazel Two.
"Greetings, Hazel!" said Hazel Three.

Hazel Two headed to the laundry room, where she accidentally turned the family's clothing purple. Hazel Three started on the washing-up.

"What a nice surprise!" said Hazel's mum. "My Little Charmer is being a *big* help!"

Hazel's dad joined them. His clothes had all turned purple in Hazel Two's laundry! He looked surprised to see Hazel in the kitchen.

"Hazel? But you were just in the laundry room," he sputtered. "I need my eyes checked!"

"Or your glasses cleaned," Hazel's mum said with a smile.

Hazel Three shook her bottle of washing-up liquid. "Out of bubbles! I must get more."

So she decided to copy herself and send Hazel Four to the shop.

But even with more washing-up liquid, everything still seemed dirty. Hazel Four needed more copies if she was really going to get *everything* clean!

A-bibbity whirl! Make an exact copy of this girl!

Now there were four more copies!

"Hazels, you will spread out and clean everything," said Hazel Four.

She handed each Hazel a bottle of washing-up liquid. Then she headed back to the shop for more.

When Posie's brother, Parsley, saw Hazel Four walking by, he thought she'd bought *too* much washing-up liquid.

"What are you going to do? Wash the whole town?" he joked.

Hazel Four looked at him with wide, blank eyes. "Yes, that is the plan."

Parsley shrugged, hopped on his broom and zoomed away.

But a moment later, he spotted Hazel cleaning the fountain. He couldn't believe his eyes. How could she have got there so fast?

"But you were—" He shook his head. "Okay, no more Sugar Fairy Frosties before bed. They make me see double!"

The next morning, the Little Charmers woke up bright and early.

"Let's have another pillow fight to see who has to make breakfast," said Lavender.

But Hazel noticed something strange. Hundreds of bubbles were floating past the Charmhouse window.

"I should probably go home to check on myself," she told her friends.

As the real Hazel drew closer to home, she noticed the fountain was frothy with soap bubbles. Then she spotted another Hazel flooding the lawn with water!

"What are you doing?" she cried.

"I am cleaning the dirt out of this garden," Hazel Nine replied.

"Gardens are supposed to have dirt!" said Hazel.

Hazel Nine shrugged. "Dirt is dirty. And you said to clean everything."

Just then, Hazel spotted her father and Parsley heading towards them.

"Snapdragons! Stay here," she told Hazel Nine.

"Morning, Mr Charming. Great purple suit," said Parsley.

"Thanks! At first I wasn't happy Hazel turned all my clothes purple. But now everything matches, so getting dressed is a breeze!" said Hazel's dad. "Where did all these bubbles come from?"

"Hazel was cleaning the fountain," answered Parsley. "I guess she used too much soap."

Parsley and Mr Charming said goodbye just as Lavender and
Posie arrived.

Lavender looked around at the bubbles. "What happened?" she asked.

"The laundry was Hazel Two's fault," said Hazel Nine. "The kitchen was
Hazel Seven. I'm not sure about the fountain."

The real Hazel was worried. "How many Hazels are there?" she asked.

Hazel Nine tried counting on her fingers. Then she shrugged. "We lost count."

"What do we do now?" Lavender asked.

"There's only one thing to do," said Hazel. "I'll have to come clean and tell the truth. But first I need to collect all the 'mes'!"

"Maybe I can help with that," Posie said. She pulled out her flute.

"Sparkle up, Charmers!" cheered Hazel.

"We wave our wands . . ." said Hazel.

"We play our wands . . ." said Posie.

"We pour our special potions . . ." said Lavender.

"We sparkle up and cast a spell in a single charming motion!" all three Charmers said together.

Posie played a dazzling song. As soon as each Hazel heard the beautiful music, she joined the parade towards the real Hazel's house.

Outside the house, Hazel gathered her courage.

Her mum and dad opened the door.

"I'm sort of in a bit of trouble," Hazel told them.

Her father's eyes widened when he saw all the Hazels. "From the look of it, I'd say you're in *double* trouble, Hazel."

Hazel sighed. "I spelled a copy spell to help me clean my room."

"But I said *you* had to clean up," said her dad.

"It was me – just a copied me," Hazel replied. "And then she made a copy. And she made a copy, and—"

"Well, only *one* of you is going to clean up this mess," said her mum.

So Hazel had to clean everything herself – without any magic.

"Great job!" Lavender said when she was done.

"It looks sparkling!" said her mum. "Who wants breakfast?"

"So, Mum, have you sent the other Hazels back yet?" asked Hazel.

"Um . . ." said her mum.

Down in the kitchen, the other Hazels were busy making breakfast. Hazel Two was cooking pancakes and delivering them Frisbee-style!

"More pancakes?" she asked Hazel's dad.

"Yes, please!" he replied.

Too bad Hazel Two's aim wasn't very good!

The real Hazel wasn't worried. She had everything she could want – good food, a great family and sparktastic best friends who were always there for her!